The Hospital

Graeme Beals

PINNACLE PRESS

The Hospital is the fourth in a five book series. Tom is in hospital recovering from the injuries he received in the accident. Will he ever see Tammy again now?

Titles follow in this sequence:

Tom and Tammy – The Hospital
ISBN 9781906373009
Ordering Code – UK7000

Curriculum Concepts UK
The Old School
Upper High Street
Bedlinog
Mid-Glamorgan CF46 6SA

Email: orders@curriculumconcepts.co.uk
www.curriculumconcepts.co.uk

Illustrated by Ross Bennett

I open one eye.

What is this?

I open both eyes.

I am in hospital.

My head hurts.

My arm hurts.

My leg hurts too.

How did I get like this?

I try to think.

Slowly I start to remember.

Tammy was talking to the big guy.

I was jealous.

I got on the fence.

I was showing off to make Tammy
see me.

A motorbike came by fast.

I got a fright and fell onto the
road.

A car was coming.

It hit me.

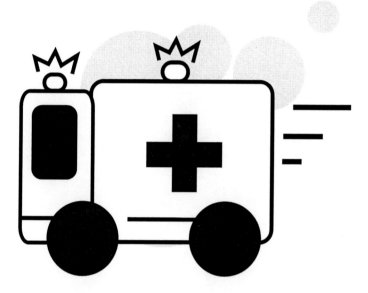

The ambulance came.

Tammy was there.

She was looking at me.

She was looking worried.

But now she will think I am stupid.

She won't want to see me again.

I feel sad and silly.

I hear a voice from the door.
"Hello Tom!"

I look around. It is Tammy.

"Hi Tammy!" I say. "It is good to
see you."

"You're lucky you can see anything," Tammy says.

"You could have been killed Tom."

"I know," I say. "I was stupid."

"Stupid . . . but nice," said Tammy.
She smiled and held my good
hand.